~FIRST GREEK MYTHS~
ARACHNE, THE SPIDER WOMAN

BY SAVIOUR PIROTTA
ILLUSTRATED BY JAN LEWIS

ORCHARD BOOKS

~ CAST LIST ~

ARACHNE
(A-rak-nee)

A clever but proud girl

ATHENA
(A-theen-a)

A great goddess

Once there was a girl called Arachne who made the most beautiful tapestries. She really was very clever!

The only trouble was, Arachne could not help showing off.

When people said, "Arachne, you weave the best tapestries in the country," Arachne would say: "How dare you? You mean I weave the best tapestries in the whole world."

And when people said, "Your work is so beautiful, Arachne. Did the goddess Athena teach you to weave?" Arachne would say:

"I taught myself to weave without any help at all, thank you!"

Late one afternoon, when
Arachne was sitting outside
working, a crowd of people
gathered round.

"I wonder what she's making
today?" said one man.

Arachne loved being the centre of attention, and she began to weave the coloured threads together even more quickly. Before long, she was holding up another stunning tapestry to the crowd.

"So it is true," cried a farmer's
wife. "Athena did teach you
to weave."

The smile disappeared from
Arachne's face.

"How many times do I have to
tell you?" she cried angrily.
"Athena did not teach me to
weave. She could never make
tapestries as beautiful as this!"

Just then an old woman dressed
in rags pushed her way to the
front of the crowd.

"Are you saying that you are
a better weaver than Athena
herself?" she asked.

"Yes!" said Arachne confidently. "And if anyone sees Athena, tell her that I challenge her to a contest."

"Very well," snapped the old lady. "Let the contest begin."

The old lady started chanting a spell and, in an instant, her hair turned from lifeless grey to dazzling, shining gold. The wrinkles disappeared from her face.

The crowd fell back.

"It can't be..." gasped a farmer.

But it was! There in front of them was the great goddess Athena herself.

"May the best weaver win," said Athena and she took a selection of brightly coloured threads and began to weave.

"I will be the best!" said Arachne
and she, too, started to weave.

In no time at all, the contest was over. Athena held up her work for the crowd to see. It was truly beautiful, with silver clouds, shooting stars and moonlit hills.

"Breathtaking," said a little old lady.

"Wonderful," agreed another man.

Then it was Arachne's turn.
With a smile on her face, she held
up her work for everyone to
admire. The crowd fell silent.

Arachne's work really was
better than Athena's.

"I told you," said Arachne, smugly. "I am by far the best weaver. You gods think you are special. Well, you are not!"

The crowd could not believe
what they were hearing. Nobody
insulted the gods like that.

"Shut up, you fool," snarled Athena. "It is true, you are the best weaver, but you have no respect for anyone. You need to be taught a lesson.

"From now on, you will only weave in the dark. No one will admire your work. Instead, they will brush it away as soon as they see it."

As Athena laughed out loud, Arachne felt a terrible pain run through her body. "What's happening?" she cried.

Everyone around her seemed to be getting bigger...

and bigger.

Then she realised, no one was getting bigger. She was getting smaller...

and smaller!

Now Athena's laugh was so loud that Arachne tried to cover her ears – but her hands had gone!

Instead she had eight long fingers, each covered in thick black hair.

Athena had turned her into
a spider!

Arachne hid under the loom,
terrified and lonely. "Will I
ever be able to weave again?"
she wondered.

When it got dark, Arachne
scuttled up a wall and started
working. She wove all through
the night, with her eight hairy
fingers.

By morning, she had spun
a beautiful web across a window.

"Look what I have made," she called to her father. But her father couldn't hear the tiny voice.

"There's a spider's web in the window," he complained to a servant. "Sweep it away now!"

Arachne ran to another corner
and started spinning a new web.
But no matter how hard she tried,
people never stopped to admire
her work again. Ever.

Poor Arachne. How she wished she had not been such a show-off, and so rude to the great goddess Athena!

~FIRST GREEK MYTHS~
ARACHNE, THE SPIDER WOMAN

BY SAVIOUR PIROTTA ⁓ ILLUSTRATED BY JAN LEWIS

And enjoy a little magic with these First Fairy Tales:

First Greek Myths and First Fairy Tales are available from all
good bookshops,or can be ordered direct from the publisher:
Orchard Books, PO BOX 29, Douglas IM99 1BQ
Credit card orders please telephone 01624 836000
or fax 01624 837033
or e-mail: bookshop@enterprise.net for details.

To order please quote title, author and ISBN
and your full name and address.
Cheques and postal orders should be
made payable to 'Bookpost plc'.
Postage and packing is FREE within the UK
(overseas customers should add £1.00 per book).

Prices and availability are subject to change.